Everything I Know

BY

CLAUDIA RECINOS SELDEEN

An imprint of Enslow Publishing

WEST **44** BOOKS™

Please visit our website, www.west44books.com.
For a free color catalog of all our high-quality books,
call toll free 1-800-398-2504.

Cataloging-in-Publication Data

Names: Seldeen, Claudia Recinos.
Title: Everything I know / Claudia Recinos Seldeen.
Description: New York : West 44, 2024. | Series: West 44 YA verse
Identifiers: ISBN 9781978596771 (pbk.) | ISBN 9781978596764
(library bound) | ISBN 9781978596788 (ebook)
Subjects: LCSH: American poetry--21st century. |
Poetry, Modern--21st century.| Poetry.
Classification: LCC PS584.S453 2024 | DDC 811.008'09282--dc23

First Edition

Published in 2024 by
Enslow Publishing LLC
2544 Clinton Street
Buffalo, NY 14224

Editor: Caitie McAneney
Designer: Leslie Taylor

Photo Credits: Cover (girl) Tenstudio/Shutterstock.com, (confusion
scribbles) Smilingirida/Shutterstock.com (various background
objects) Malysheva Anastasiia & HelenField/Shutterstock.com.

Printed in the United States of America

CPSIA compliance information: Batch #CS24W44: For further information contact
Enslow Publishing LLC at 1-800-398-2504.

For my family

Home

Mom once said,
Home is where the heart is.

But the heart is just an organ.
A pumping machine.

I think
home
is where I can look out
the same window
every day.
And see the same trees.
The same sunrise.
The same sky.

Home
is where my routines
are safe.

Where I can follow them
like a line
on the palm of my hand.

Like a
heartbeat.

Steady
and
dependable.

The Rainbow

My dad
told me I was autistic
when I was eight years old.

*Everyone's brain is
different,
he said.
Like a rainbow.*

*Some people
are all the way over
in the red.*
       *Some people
       are in the middle.*
*And others
are at the opposite end.
With the blues.
And the violets.*

Since that day,
I've learned lots of words
to explain my autism.
       Neural development.
       Spectrum Disorder.

But my favorite explanation
will always be
the rainbow.

One Step at a Time

The halls
get crowded
between classes.

Elbows bump.
Kids shout.
Lockers slam.

Each sound
is an electric shock.
A snap.
Like a rubber band.

I ground myself
by putting on
my headphones.
To block out
the noise.

I ground myself
by counting
my steps.

It takes 408 steps
to get from
one end
of the school
to the other.

It takes 204 steps
to get from third period
to fourth.

I know
this school.

I know
this path.

So I take it
one step
at a time.

Chris

Chris is sitting in the grass
at our usual lunch spot.

His brown hair hangs
like a curtain
over one eye.

His smile
is the same smile
I've seen
every
day
since I turned five.

He looks up
and waves.

And I stop counting
my steps.

Birthday

Some things
are easy.

When I turned five,
my mom
baked a chocolate cake.

My dad
strung lights
on our back porch.

They took me outside
and sang
"Happy Birthday."

I stared at the
bright
yellow
flicker
of my candles.
Trying hard to remember
not to touch.

Halfway through the song,
Chris
walked into our backyard.

His bangs
were in his eyes.

His Captain America T-shirt
was inside out.

But his smile
was just as bright
as my birthday candles.

I'm your neighbor,
he said.
My name's Chris.

And
that
was
it.

We've been
best friends
ever since.

Ten
years.

One
decade.

As easy
as chocolate cake.

As easy
as turning five.

Tuesday

I sit
on the grass
next to Chris.

Instead of saying,
Hello,
he hands me
his peanut butter cookies.

Instead of saying,
How are you?
I hand him
my grapes.

We've been having the same
silent conversation
since fourth grade.
Since I told my mom
I don't like foods that
pop
and
squish
in my mouth.
And she
didn't listen.

*Can I come over
after school?*
Chris asks.

I shake my head.
It's Tuesday.

He pops a grape
in his mouth.

*I need help
with math,*
he says.

It's Tuesday,
I say.
Louder,
in case he didn't hear me.
*Physics club
meets on Tuesdays.*

Chris shrugs.
*I just thought
you could skip a day, Mia.*

I look up at him,
eyes wide.

Are you crazy?
I cry.

He tosses
a grape
at
me.

I throw a cookie
at
him.

And then we're both
laughing.

Heads
thrown back.

Leaning
into
each
other.

Like we
always do.

Everything I Know

There's a white mailbox
in front of our house.
Dad painted
our name
on it
in black letters
before I was born.

G U T I E R R E Z.

This is our house,
he tells me
whenever I ask about it.
It should have
a name tag.

I've lived
in this house
my whole life.
I know the way
the wind chime
on the porch
sings.
The way the driveway
dips.

I know the way
Chris's yard
presses up to mine.
I see the paving stones
leading up to his door.

And I know
exactly
which one I tripped over
when I was seven.
I look at his porch swing.
And I remember
the day
he told me
his parents were getting
divorced.

I know
it takes me
nine minutes
to walk home
from school.
Every day.

Nine minutes.
Five blocks.
That's 1,180 steps.

And
then,
I'm home.

Hugs

Where's my hug?
Mom asks
when she sees me.

I stand very still
and let her put her arms
around me.

Even though
her perfume
tickles my nose.

Even though
she's wearing her
scratchy sweater.

Dad never asks for hugs.
He asks for fist bumps.
Our knuckles touch
and then drift away.
Like atoms crashing
in space.

But Mom
is always saying,
You have to be strong.

Mom
likes hugs.

And asking
how my day was.

And packing grapes
in my lunch.

Poetry

Mom
teaches college classes.
Just like Dad.

Dad teaches physics.
Numbers and math.

But Mom
teaches
English.

She's always
bringing home
books
of poetry.
Reading them to me.
Trying to get me to
see
what she
sees.

I like words
sometimes.
When they're about
science.

But Mom's poetry
is never
about science.

Mom's poetry
is slippery
like wet grass.

It hardly
ever
rhymes.

And it never
makes any
sense.

Numbers

Chris and I
sit in my room.
On the beanbags
Dad gave me
for Christmas.

I push Chris's math book
toward him.
But he pushes it
back.

Algebra
doesn't make
sense!
he cries.

I
frown.

Numbers
aren't like
words.
Or poems.

Numbers are
exactly
what they seem
to be.

I take
a deep breath.
And I remind myself
of all the ways
being friends with
Chris
is easy.

1. He doesn't make me talk
   about things
   I don't like.
   Like football.
   Or music.

2. He lets me talk
   about physics.
   About energy.
   And light.

3. And he never
   rolls his eyes.
   He never
   gets
   bored.

I pick up
Chris's math book.

Look,
I say.
*It makes
perfect sense.*

And then,
I explain it again.

Slowly.

One
step
at
a
time.

Tonight

Chris usually stays
for dinner.

But
tonight,
Mom shakes her head.

Tonight,
it's just
Mom and Dad and me.

Just the three of us.
At our tiny
kitchen table.

News

Your mom
and I
have news,
Dad announces.

He takes a deep breath
and looks
at Mom.

She looks back at him
and nods.

I can tell
something big
is coming.
So I grip my fork tight.
Like I'm holding on
to a rope.

I got a new job,
Dad says.

In
Boston.

We're
moving
to Boston.

Boston

The word
Boston
is heavy.

Two bursts
of sound.

Like two cracks
of thunder.

I'm not sure
I heard right.
So I ask,
What do you mean?

Mom rakes her hands
through her dark curls.

She looks
at Dad.

She looks
at me.

*It means
you'll have to
be strong,
Mia,*
she says.

*We're leaving
Kansas City.*

*We're moving
away.*

Six States

I look out
the window
and see:

1. Chris's house.

2. Chris's dining room
   window.

3. Chris's yard
   next to mine.

I close my eyes
and picture
Kansas City
on a map.

I picture
Boston.

There are
six states
between them.

We're moving
half a dozen states
away.

Niña Mía

That night,
Dad knocks
on my bedroom door.
Soft knocks.
Like tree branches
tapping
against one another.

I'm here,
he says.
If you want
to talk.

I pull
the bedsheets
over my head.
I don't want to move
to Boston.

Dad
sighs.

Niña mía,
he says.

My
girl . . .

Things Change

My name,
Mia,
means
mine
in Spanish.

So Dad calls me
Niña mía
when I'm angry.
Or when I'm sad.

He whispers,
Niña mía.
And I smile.

But tonight,
Dad says,
Niña mía,
I know
you don't want
to move.

But
sometimes,
things change.

Even if
you don't want
them to.

Three Letters

Dad
tells me
about Boston.

Harvard
Square.
       Fenway
       Park.
              Boston
              Harbor.

Places
he says
I'll love.

But
the words
mean nothing
to me.

They're just
sounds.

Why do we have to move?
I ask.

Dad's glasses
catch the moonlight.
They wink and shine.

Because
I got a new job,
he says.
At MIT.

MIT.
Massachusetts
Institute of
Technology.

It's one of the
best
schools
for physics.

Dad says
that word.
Those three
letters.

M
    I
        T

And something sparks
like electricity
in my heart.

Physics

When I turned nine,
my babysitter
caught the flu.

Mom was working
on her master's degree.
Swimming through
books
and
books
of poetry.

So, Dad took me
to work
with him.

At first,
I was mad.

I didn't like the dim light
in his classroom.
Or the way his students
stared.

I was annoyed
by the hum
of the air conditioning.
And the sharp smell
of dry-erase markers.

But
then,
Dad walked to the front
of the room.
He wrote
an equation
on the board.

Letters.
Arrows.
Numbers.

I forgot about
the air conditioning.
And the markers.
And the other students.

I think I even
forgot
to breathe.

Everything
Dad wrote
on the board
was neat and tidy.
Like puzzle pieces
finding their home.

Everything
Dad wrote
made
sense.

Any Time You Want

Dad sits
on the edge
of my bed.
A gentle weight.
Like an anchor.

*I know this move
will be hard,*
he says.
*But
this is a great job.
I'll be the new dean
of the physics department
at MIT.*

A thought blooms
in my head.
Like a flower.

*Can I watch
you teach?*
I ask.

Dad's glasses
gleam.
*Any time
you want,*
he says.

I flap
my hands.
A thing I do
when I'm
feeling
too much.
When I have to
let
the feeling
out.

Some people
call it
stimming.

I call it
letting my hands
dance.

Dad waits
until my hands
have settled.
Then he says,
You know that book
I gave you
when you turned twelve?

I scowl.
Of course I know.
It was the first book
about physics
I ever read.

The book
that made me see
how everything
can be solved
with science.
You just have to be
patient.
You just have to try.

Dad leans
forward.

Well,
he says.
*The author of that book
works at MIT.*

*You'll be able
to meet
Dr. Patel.*

*Any
time
you
want.*

Lists

I lie awake.
Long after Dad leaves.
Long after the house
grows quiet.
I lie in the dark.
And I make lists.

Like I always do
when I'm
stressed out.

One list
is about home.

1. My room
2. My school
3. Chris

The other list
is about
Boston.

1. Watching Dad teach
2. Dr. Patel
3. MIT
4. MIT
5. MIT . . .

Waves

The next day,
I meet Chris
at our usual
lunch spot.

He smiles
when he sees me.

He lifts
his hand
and waves.

I wave back
at him.

But
I
don't
smile.

I Have News, Too

Chris pops grapes
in his mouth.
One at a time.
Like he's feeding coins
into a parking meter.

I have news!
he tells me.
I got
a B
on my math quiz!

He grins.
And his hand
goes up
for a fist bump.

Usually,
I'd bump his fist
with mine.

And then I'd tell him
he should have gotten
an A.

But
today,
I don't do that.

Today,
I shake my head.

And when Chris frowns,
I say,
I have news, too.

I Know

I'm moving away,
I tell Chris.
We're moving to Boston.

Chris makes a soft sound.
Like he's
blowing out
a birthday candle.

Mia . . .
he says.

I nod
and look away.

Chris and I
have been having
silent conversations
for years.

I know
when he says,
Mia . . .

He means,
*Everything
is going
to change.*

I know
he means,
*What will I do
without you?*

I know
he's saying,
*I don't want you
to go.*

Unstuck

At the end
of the week,
I clean out
my locker.

Textbooks.
Pencils.
A candy bar wrapper
from last Halloween.
I stuff it all
in my backpack.

My locker stands
empty.
Clean.
Except
for the sticker
Chris gave me
for Christmas.
The one I
stuck
just inside
my locker door.

It's a picture
of an atom.
And underneath,
it says:
YOU MATTER!

I run my fingers
over the peeling edges.
And I realize
I won't be able
to unstick it.

I won't be able
to take it
with me.

I'll have to leave it
behind.

Ready to Go

Chris and I walk home
together
after school.
When we reach
the corner,
I push the crosswalk button.

But Chris flops down
on the sidewalk.

Are you okay?
I ask.

Chris winds his fingers
in his shoelaces.
He takes a deep breath.
And lets out
one
long
sigh.

You don't seem
upset
about moving,
he says.
You seem like you're
ready
to
go.

Knots

In first grade,
I got glue
all over
my fingers.

We weren't allowed
to wash our hands.
Not until art time
was over.

So I tried
to ignore
the way the glue
tightened my skin.
The fuzz of dust
sticking
to my fingertips.

But the more
I tried to ignore it,
the louder
it felt.

So
I started
to cry.
And cry.
And cry.

Dad said
crying
was how I talked
to everyone.
How I told them
something
was wrong.

But Mom said,
You have to be strong.

So I learned
to tie my feelings
up
in knots.

To hide
them.

I learned
how to be
strong.

I Try

I try to tell Chris
about my lists.
About Dr. Patel.
About MIT.

I try to tell him
about my
knots.

But Chris doesn't
look up.

He keeps playing
with his shoelaces.

And I know
he doesn't
understand.

Today

My alarm goes off
at 6 a.m.
Just like
it always
does.

Mom comes
breezing
into my nearly empty room.
A smile
tacked onto her face.

Moving truck made it to Boston.
Are you ready
for moving day?
she asks.

I look out the window.
And see the same trees.
The same sunrise.
The same sky.

I take a deep breath.
And I tie all my worries up.
All my sadness.
All my fear.

I tell Mom
I'm ready.

Porch Steps

Chris is sitting
on our porch
when it's time to go.

Dad gives me
a quick pat
on the shoulder.

*We'll wait
in the car,*
he says.

Then he follows Mom
down the porch steps.

Leaving
me and Chris
alone.

Goodbye

I look out
over our front lawn.

I see:

1. The edge
   of the porch.
   Where Chris and I
   carved our initials.

2. The tree
   he fell out of
   when he was eight.

3. The gardenia bush
   that makes him sneeze
   every spring.

Everything I see
brings me
back
to this moment.
To my
best friend.
To Chris.

I close my eyes.
And think of
physics.
Of particles bumping
into each other.
And then spinning away.

Goodbye, Mia,
Chris says.

His voice sounds small.
Like we're already
miles apart.

I want to tell Chris
I'm going to miss him.

But I know
I have to be
brave.

I can't take Chris
with me.

I have to leave him
behind.

So I squeeze my hands
into fists.

I brush Chris's knuckles
with mine.

And then I force myself
to spin away.

42 Steps

There are
42 steps
from our front porch
to the driveway.

I count
each
one.

And then I'm in
the taxi.

It smells like air freshener.
Like toasted marshmallows.

We're backing
out.

And there's
nothing
left
to count.

Life Jacket

At the airport,
I pop
my headphones
over my ears.

Everything goes soft.
Muffled.

Like
        gently
                rocking
                        waves.

My headphones
are a life jacket.

They keep
my head
above water.

With my headphones on,
I can move
with the crowd.
I can move
through the line.

I can move
just like
everyone else does.

How's Boston?

The drive
from the airport
feels long.

Especially
after a morning
full of plane rides.

I stretch my arms
over my head.
I roll my wrists
and ankles.
Sometimes,
s t r e t c h i n g
steadies the nervous knocking
of my heart.
The restless
tap tap tap
of impatience.

My phone
buzzes
in my back pocket.
Telling me I have
a new message.

How's Boston?
Chris writes.

I type back,
It's okay.

Outside,
a river unfolds.
Steel blue.

*I wish
you were here,*
I start to type.

But before
I can finish,
Dad lifts one arm.
He points
straight ahead.

There it is,
he says.
Our new house!

New House

Our new house
isn't as big
as our old house.

But there's a porch
that wraps around
the side.
There's a long,
straight driveway.
And
in my bedroom,
there's a window
that takes up
a whole wall.

*This is where
we'll put
your telescope,*
Dad says.

I look out
the window.
Up at the sky.
And I imagine
a night
full of stars.
Just waiting
to be seen.

Mom

That night,
Mom comes into
my room.
Her skirt sweeping
around her ankles.

When I was little,
Dad used to teach
night school.
He would come home
long after
I'd gone to bed.

So Mom was the one
who would brush
my teeth.
Who would read
me stories.
Who would tuck
me in.

Mom's bare feet
pad
on the carpet.
Whisper soft.
Like the wind
against my window.

She sits
on the edge of my bed.
And I remember
how she used to
snuggle
under the covers
beside me.
How she would
read me
funny stories.
Poetry.
Full of silly words
that filled her mouth
like jellybeans.

Mom tucks a strand
of my hair
behind my ear.
And I wonder
if she'd still
tell me a story.
If I asked.

She presses a kiss
to my forehead.

Get some sleep, Mia.
she says.
*Don't forget
you have school
tomorrow.*

Stars

I lie awake
long after Mom leaves.

I stare
out the window.
And watch the clouds
move over the stars.

It makes me feel
better
to know
they are still there.

Even when
they're hidden.

Even when
I can't
see them.

Strong, Mia

My school in Kansas City
was only five blocks
away.

But
my new school
is farther.
Too many blocks.
Too far to walk.

I sit in the car
with Mom.
The radio singing.
My backpack
at my feet.

When we pull up
in front of the school,
my heart flutters.

I look up
at the big
gray building.
At the stream
of kids
walking in.

So many
unfamiliar faces.

A sob
tightens my throat.

But Mom puts her hand
over mine.

Strong, Mia,
she says.

So I bite back
the urge
to cry.

I lift my chin.
I take a deep breath.
And I step out
of the car.

Inside

The inside of the school
is a live wire.

People zip past me.
An electric current.
A door slams.
A bell rings.
Someone screams with laughter.

I think about putting on
my headphones.

But then I decide
against it.

Being autistic is mine.
My information.
To share
when I am ready.

And I'm not
ready.

So, I decide to leave
my headphones
in my bag.

Instead,
I count my steps.
One
after
the
other.

I make my way
through the crowded halls.

Biology

My first class is
biology.
The study of
living things.

It's not physics.
But at least
it's science.

Our teacher's name
is Ms. Fray.
Her hair is white.
Like dandelion fluff.

She calls my name.
Mia Gutierrez.

I raise my hand.
And she smiles.

*Mia
is our new student,*
she announces.

*I know you will all
make her feel
welcome.*

Locker

My new locker
is empty.
No candy wrappers
inside.
No spare pencils.
It's a blank canvas.
A blank sheet of paper.
Waiting to be filled.

I touch the spot
where Chris's sticker
would be.
Where it probably
still is.
In my old locker.
In my old school.

The knot
inside my heart
unwinds a little.

So I grit my teeth.
I count to 10.
Then 20.
Then 50.

You have to be brave,
I tell myself.
You have to be strong.

My Spot

At lunchtime,
I sit on the grass.
Under a tree
with no leaves.

I look up
at the bare branches.
And I wonder
if Chris
is doing the same.
If he's sitting
in our old lunch spot.
By himself.
Just like me.

Hi,
a voice says
behind me.

I turn
and see
a girl
standing over me.
A brown paper bag
in her hands.

You're in my spot,
she says.

My heart
d
  i
    p
     s.

But then,
she shakes her head.

She tucks
a sleek wisp
of hair
behind her ear.
And I notice her nails
are painted
dark blue.

She sits down
beside me.
Legs crossed
like mine.

We have biology together,
she says.
My name is Tova.

Just Like Chris

Tova's hair
is like spilled ink.
A pool of black
over her shoulders.

She laughs
when I tell her
I'm from Kansas City.

But
when I hold out
my grapes,
she frowns.

What's wrong with them?
she asks.

I don't like them,
I explain.

Tova's black-lined eyes
narrow.

But then, she shrugs.
She takes the bag.

Just like Chris
used to do.

English

I have
English
next.

Our teacher,
Ms. Levin,
has us open our books.
Right to the middle.
To a poem
that doesn't rhyme.

I look down
at the words
and sigh.

Poetry
is slippery.
Like dish soap.
Like our driveway
when it ices over
in winter.

Poetry
is a lot
like grapes
packed in lunch bags.
And hugs.
And Mom.

Today Is the Day

Dad picks me up
after school.

Today is the day
I get to see his new office.
His new lab.
Today is the day
I get to see
MIT.

The Physics Building

Dad works in a tall,
narrow building.

The physics building,
he tells me.
Where all the
physics labs
are.

I imagine walking
into one of the
research rooms.
Slipping on
a lab coat.
Taking out
a notebook
and
a pen.

The thought
makes me smile.

The thought
makes my hands
dance and flutter.
Like butterflies
that have been
set free.

Shall We?

At the end
of a long hall,
Dad stops.

Niña mía,
he says.
*This is
Dr. Patel's lab.*

He tips his head
and asks,
*Shall we go
inside?*

Dr. Patel

There's a picture
of Dr. Patel
on the back of his book.
(The book
Dad gave me
when I turned 12.)

In the picture,
Dr. Patel's hair
is silver.
And his thick eyebrows
are pulled in.
Like ropes
knotted together.

The real Dr. Patel
doesn't look
like knotted ropes.

The real Dr. Patel
reminds me of
winking stars.

Dark eyes
flicker merrily
under bushy brows.
White teeth flash
in a wide smile.

Hello, Dr. Gutierrez,
he says to Dad.

He takes Dad's thin hand
in his larger one.
He gives it
several
hearty shakes.

And then
he turns
to me.

This is my daughter,
Dad says.
This is Mia.

It's very nice
to meet you,
Mia,
Dr. Patel says.

Welcome
to my lab.

A Short Tour

Dr. Patel's lab
is bright.
Not the harsh light
of overhead bulbs.
But the warm glow
of reading lamps.
Of fireplaces.
Of afternoon sunshine.

In my lab,
Dr. Patel tells us,
we study
atoms
and
molecules.

He stops
next to a workbench.
He waves
his hand
over knobs
and sensors.
Glass lenses.
Green wires.

I'm interested
in photons.
he says.

His gaze lands
on me.
And the corners
of his eyes
crinkle.

*Do you know
what photons are?*
he asks.

I nod.

Of course
I know.

*Photons are
particles
of light,*
I say.

That's right!
Dr. Patel cries.
Very good.

Happiness
pops and shimmers
inside me.
Like fireworks.

I force myself
to wait
until Dr. Patel
turns around.

And then
I let my hands
wing
and
twirl
around me.

Niels

There's a small office
at the back
of Dr. Patel's lab.

Someone is sitting
at the desk
inside.
Head bent
over a laptop.
Headphones
on his ears.

This is my son,
Dr. Patel tells us.
This is Niels.

Niels looks
like he's my age.
Maybe a little
older.

He has
Dr. Patel's eyes.
Dark and glittering.

But Dr. Patel's hair
is silver.
And Niels's hair
is glossy and black.
Like raven feathers.

His hair
makes me think of
crisp breezes.
Crows sitting in
tree branches.
Rustling wings.

It's nice to meet you, Niel,
Dad says.

Niels,
Dr. Patel corrects.
With an s at the end.

Like the scientist, I say.
Niels Bohr.

Dr. Patel's eyes
gleam.

That's exactly right!
he says.

My hands flit
through the air.
A quick dance.
Before I catch myself.

Before I
shove them
in my pockets.

But not before
Niels sees.

Me Too

Dr. Patel says,
Niels,
why don't you show Mia
the student lounge?

So I follow Niels
out of the lab.
Down the hallway.
Up the stairs.
And into a small room
with yellow walls.

Tables and couches
crowd together.
Vending machines
hum
against the wall.

This is
the lounge,
Niels says.

His voice
is soft.
Whispery.
And I have to
lean in
to hear him.

I turn
in a slow circle.

I imagine myself
slipping in here.
Taking a break
from a day
of research.
I picture myself
falling onto one of the
brown leather couches.
My head spinning
with equations.
Numbers.
Math.

I turn back
and look at Niels.

But Niels
is looking at
my hands.
Watching them
fly
in the air
beside me.

I fold my hands
to my chest.
Embarrassed.

I'm autistic,
I explain.

Niels looks at me.
His eyes as dark
as night skies.
His gaze
hovers
somewhere
around my chin.
And he says,
Me too.

Like Me

When Niels smiles,
his whole face
lights up.
Like a lantern
flaring to life.

When Niels smiles,
I realize
I've never had
an autistic
friend
before.

Someone with
challenges.
Like mine.

Someone with
stories.
Like mine.

Someone
to complain
and celebrate
with.

Someone
like
me.

A Job

Back in the lab,
Dr. Patel announces
that he needs a
research assistant.

Mia,
he says.
*How would you like
a job?*

I picture myself
coming into Dr. Patel's lab.
Playing with magnets
and electricity.
Studying light.

I see myself
walking into Dr. Patel's office.
Waving at Dr. Patel.
Waving at Niels.

I bounce
up and down
on my toes.

I look at Dr. Patel.
And I say,
Yes!

Text

Chris texts me
right before bed.

How was your day?
he asks.

I start to tell him about MIT.
About school.
About Niels.
But then,
I stop.

Telling Chris about
my day
makes me realize
he's not part of it.
Not anymore.

So I don't tell him
everything.

I tell him
one word.

Good.

And then I
set my phone
aside.

Each Number

The hallways
at my new school
are always crowded.

The noise buzzes
around my head.
Like swarming bees.

I ground myself
by counting.

There are 92 steps
from the front door
to my locker.

There are 180 steps
from my locker
to first period.

I repeat each number
softly
to myself.

I tuck each number
away.

I learn my way
around the school.
One step
at a time.

Favorite

I walk into biology.
And I see Tova.
Front and center.

Her hair is roped
into two sleek braids.

Her nails are painted
green.

*I always try
to sit up front,*
she tells me.
*Biology
is my favorite.*

My heart swells.
Like a hot-air balloon.

I fold my hands together
to keep them from
dancing.

Me too,
I say.
I like science, too.

Research Assistant

After school,
I drive with Dad
to MIT.

Dr. Patel smiles
when I walk in.
He waves me in and says,
Welcome!

I join him
at his workbench.
And he dives
into an explanation
of his work.

Light scattering.
Photons.
Energy.

The words bounce
around the room.

Words I learned
from his book.

Words that
come together
like notes
to make a song.

Background Reading

Dr. Patel
clears a space
for me
in his back office.

He sets a stack
of papers
down.
He claps
his hands
and smiles.

Background reading,
he says.
Very important.

When he leaves,
I look over at Niels.

My eyes trip over
his laptop.
His headphones.
The soft feather
of his ink-colored hair.

He glances at me.
And his mouth curves
in a slow smile.

We work quietly
for the rest
of the afternoon.

Heads
bent.

Brows
furrowed.

We don't say
a word.
But we sit
together.
Side
by
side.

I Brought You Something

Dad comes into my room
right before bed.

Niña Mia,
he says.
*I brought you
something.*

He hands me
what looks like
a notebook.
But thinner.
Flatter.

It's a calendar,
he tells me.
*From the MIT
bookstore.*

He flips it open
to the right month.
Then he pins it
to my wall.

*So you can
keep track
of your new
schedule,*
he tells me.

*So you can make
a new routine.*

Three Afternoons

After Dad leaves,
I push my covers back.
And I slide
out of bed.

I pick up
a black marker.
And I mark off
three afternoons
each week.

The three afternoons
I go to MIT.

The three afternoons
I am
a research assistant.

I can do this.

A Heartbeat

Ms. Fray
puts a drawing
of a heart
up on the board.
And she tells us about
blood flow.
Blood cells.
Oxygen.

All the things
we need
to live and breathe.

I look over
and see Tova
frowning.

Her dark hair
is pulled back
in a ponytail.

Her nails
are painted
orange.

Her pen
tap tap taps
against her notebook.

You sound
like a heartbeat,
I whisper.
Tova looks over at me.
Her pen freezes
in her hand.
And for a moment,
I wonder
if I've said something
wrong.

But then
she laughs out loud.

I hold my breath
and look at Ms. Fray.

But Ms. Fray
just goes on talking.
Her pointer
moving over
the four chambers
of the heart.

I'll See You

Tova walks with me
after first period.

I do my best
to ignore
the buzz
of hallway noise.
To listen to Tova.
To focus.

But it's hard
to find Tova's voice
in the sea of sound.

At my locker,
Tova says,
I'll see you at lunch.

I nod and say,
Okay.

She laughs.
Nose crinkling.
And then she walks
away.

Every Day

I wake up
every
day
at 6 a.m.

Mom drives me
to school.
Past trimmed lawns.
Wooden porches.

I count my steps
from class to class.
Biology.
English.
Math.

At lunchtime,
I sit with Tova
on the grass.
I lean back
and listen to her
talk about science.
About organisms
and living systems.

At work,
Dr. Patel shows me
how to use
a photon detector.

To count particles of light.
I slip into the back office.
And sit next to Niels.
And I read article
after article.

The days take shape
one by one.
Like ocean waves
growing quiet.
Like glitter in a snow globe.
Settling softly.

The World Goes Quiet

On my way
to English one day,
I try to count
my steps.

Like I've been doing
every day.

But the noise
is louder than usual.
It drowns out
my thoughts.
It swallows them
whole.

I reach
into my backpack.
I pull out
my headphones.

Being autistic is mine.
To share
when I'm ready.
And I feel ready.

So I put my
headphones on.

And the world
goes quiet.

The World Explodes

With my headphones on,
everything is muffled.
Muted.
I feel protected.
Like I'm inside
a bubble.

I walk
101 steps
from my locker
to class.

I step
through the doorway.
My eyes
on my feet.

And then someone
snatches
my headphones.
Right off my head.

And the world
explodes
into sound.

Staring

Ms. Levin,
my English teacher,
holds
my headphones
in her hand.

No electronics
in my class,
she says.

She tucks my headphones
inside her desk drawer.
She pulls her eyebrows
together
in a hard line.

You can get these back
in the main office,
she tells me.

I open my mouth
to argue.
To tell her
I need them.

My headphones
are my life jacket!
My life raft . . .

But then
I realize
everything
has gone
silent.

I look around
and see
everyone staring.
Eyes like pins.

I snap my mouth
closed.

I duck
my head.
And I don't say
anything
at all.

One Word

For the rest
of second period,
I sit in my chair.
My eyes on my book.
My hands folded tight.

Ms. Levin
reads us a poem.
Her voice rising
and falling.
Like the pitch
of a boat
on a stormy sea.

What do you think
this poem is about?
she asks.

I look down
at my textbook.
And I try to find meaning
in the lines
on the page.

But there's only
one word in my head.
Headphones.
Ringing out
like a bell.

How Was School?

Dad picks me up
after school.

I climb into
the car.
And the toasted sugar
smell
of the air freshener
fills my nose.

How was school?
he asks.

I shake
my head.

Dad
is usually
the one person
I can talk to.
The one person
who listens.

But
I don't want
to tell him
about my missing
headphones.

Talking about it
will make my stomach
dive.
Like it's happening
all over
again.

So I turn my head.
I look out
the window.

I watch the cars
slip by.
Like bubbles
in a stream.

Algebra Is the Worst!

That night
Chris
texts me.

*I got a C
on my math test.*

*Algebra is
the worst!*

I think of
the last time
Chris sat
in my room.
How he
pushed
his algebra book
away.
How I
pushed it
back.

I know
when Chris says
*Algebra is
the worst*,
he wants me
to argue.

He wants me
to text him.

But I'm still thinking
about my headphones.
My thoughts
are a nervous loop.
I couldn't break free
if I tried.

What if
my headphones
are lost
forever?

What if
I can't
get them back?

Another Day

I wake up.
And for a moment,
I forget
I'm in Boston.
I think I'm back
in Kansas City.

For
       just
one
       minute
I think
today
is Tuesday.
And Tuesday
means physics club!

But
then,
I remember.

There's no
physics club
at my new school.

And today
isn't Tuesday,
anyway.

This Is Me

The drive to school
is quiet.

Mom hums softly
to herself.
But I look out
the window.
I count the cars
going by.
So I don't have to
think about
gathering up
my courage.
Going into
the office.
Getting my headphones
back.

When we get
to school,
I hesitate.

I want to tell Mom
what happened.
I want to tell her
I feel sick.
I want to ask
for help.

But Mom
pats my hand.
Before I can say
anything.

It's just school, Mia,
she says.
You can do this.
Just be brave.

I take a deep breath.
And force myself
to step out
of the car.

I don't tell her
this is me
being brave.

This is me.
This is me.
This is me.

Sound

I make my way
to the main office.
Slowly.
Like I'm dragging
my feet
through drifts of snow.

The usual
hallway noise
swims
around me.
Books hitting
locker shelves.
Voices
bouncing
against the walls.

It's almost all
drowned out
by the sound of my own
scared heartbeat.

I'm Autistic

The woman
at the front desk
holds
my headphones
up.

*I can't give these
back,*
she says.
*Not until
the end
of the day.*

I think of
all the noise
in the hallway.
Shouts and echoes.
Screeching bells.
Banging doors.
And my heart
knocks
against my chest.

*I need
my headphones,*
I say.
*To shut
the noise
out.*

Her thin brows
come together.

I need them,
I explain.

Because
I'm
autistic . . .

Watching

The woman's cheeks
turn dark red.
Like the grapes
Mom packs in my lunch
each day.

She hands me
my headphones.
And I hurry
out of the office.

But not before I see
two girls
I recognize
from my biology class.
Their heads
turning
to follow me.
Their eyes
round and wide.

Whispers

The whispers start
after third period.

I catch words
here and there.
Like snatching fruit flies
out of the air.
Autistic.
            Headphones.
Office.

The whispers
follow me
in the hall.
To my locker.

The whispers
circle and buzz
around my head
all morning.

At Lunchtime

At lunchtime
I sit alone
on the grass.
Under a tree
with no leaves.

I close my eyes
and lift my face
up to the sun.

I hear
the grass rustling.
The high-pitched cry
of a bird.

Laughter . . .

I open
my eyes.

I look over
my shoulder.
And I see Tova.
Sitting with a group
I don't recognize.
Four of them
in a circle.
Like points
on a compass.

Tova's eyes
catch mine.
So I lift my hand
and wave.

But one of her friends
leans over.
She whispers
in Tova's ear.
And Tova's cheeks
turn pink.

She looks at me.
And her mouth
twists up
in a half-hearted smile.

But she doesn't
wave back.

Back into the School

I throw
my lunch bag
in my backpack.
Even though
I barely touched it.

I get up
and walk back
into the school.

They Knew Me

The hallways
are humming
with noise.

So I put
my headphones
on.

Everything goes
flat.
Like I'm swimming
underwater.

I can't hear
any whispers.

But I can feel
people staring.

I can feel their eyes.
Like headlights.
Washing over me.

I think about
my old school.
In Kansas City.
Where nobody cared
if I wore headphones.
Nobody cared
if I counted steps.

Nobody cared
that I was autistic.
Because they
knew me.

They had all
known me
since kindergarten.

I wasn't
new
to them.

That's Fine

How was your day?
Mom asks
when she picks me up.

She's sitting
behind the wheel.
Smiling at me.
Like she always does.

She reaches for me.
Arms open.
And I brace for a hug.

But all of my senses
start chattering.
Like a radio
turned up
too high.

I pull away.
Out of her reach.

*I don't want
a hug,*
I tell her.

Silence
fills the car.

Okay,
Mom says.
Her voice is tight.
Like a violin string.

That's fine,
she says.

And then she doesn't say
anything else
the whole car ride home.

I Wonder

The drive home is long.
So much longer
than it was
in Kansas City.

I look out the window
and see storefronts.
Muddy sidewalks.
Houses I don't know.

I wonder
what Chris is doing.

I wonder
if he's made
a new friend.
Someone new
to walk home with.
To share his
peanut butter cookies.

Or if he's
alone.

Lonely.

Just
like
me.

?

Alone
in my room,
I pull out my phone.

I see a text from Chris.
And the knots
in my heart
twist
and
strain.

Chris doesn't say hello.
He doesn't ask
what I'm doing.
He just texts me
a question mark.
Nothing more.

Chris and I
have been having
silent conversations
for years.

I know
when he sends me
a question mark,
he's asking,
How are you?

But I know
he's also asking,
What's wrong?

I realize
it's been
days
since I talked to Chris.

I think of the last time
I saw him.
How he stood
on my porch step.
How we said
goodbye.

I want to tell Chris
about my headphones.
About Tova.

But Chris
can't help me.

Chris isn't
here.

I can't rely on Chris
anymore.

Grapes

Mom calls me
into the kitchen.

When I walk in,
I find her standing
at the counter.
Mouth pinched.
Eyebrows pinned together.
Dark curls a whirlwind
around her frowning face.

She holds up a bag
of grapes.

*I found these
in your lunch bag,*
she says.
You didn't eat them.

I stare at her.
Heart pounding.

*I don't like
grapes,*
I remind her.
*I don't like the way
they pop
in my mouth.*

Mom clucks her tongue.
Don't be silly,
she says.
You always
used to eat them
before.

The word
silly
catches in my head.
It bounces
back and forth.
Like an echo.
Like a heartbeat.

I never ate them!
I cry.
I always
gave them
to Chris.

The Same Look

Mom's breath
comes rushing out
in one big
whoosh.
And I think of
balloons
deflating.

She looks at me.
Like she always does
when I've done
something wrong.

It's the same look
Ms. Levin gave me.
When she took
my headphones away.

The same look
Tova gave me.
When her friend
whispered
in her ear.

I see Mom's eyes
glaze over.
And something inside me
falls away.

Being Me

Dad once told me
everyone was different.
Like a rainbow.

But he didn't tell me
how being different
would feel.

Like I'm always
off rhythm.
Out of sync.
Like I'm singing
in a different
key.

I'm suddenly
so
tired
of being different.

Of letting Mom
down.

Of not being
what she wants me
to be.

Mia,
Mom says.

But I cut her off
with a shake
of my head.

I know!
I shout.

I have to be
brave!

I have to be
strong!

I have to
stop
being me.

Just Like Mom

Niña mía,
Dad says later.
I heard
you got in a fight
with your mom.

We're sitting in the car.
On the way
to MIT.

I look out my window.
And see a truck
rumbling past.
But my window
is rolled up.
So I barely hear it.

Niña mía,
Dad says.
Your mom says
you shouted at her.

I shake
my head.

Dad
is usually
the one person
I can talk to.

But I can tell
by the way his shoulders
sag.
By the way his voice
tightens.
By the way
he sighs.

He's disappointed in me.
Just like Mom.

Fine

Dr. Patel waves
when I walk in.

How are you?
he asks.

When I was 10,
my parents
sent me to a coach.
To learn social skills.

I never want you
to be ashamed
of who you are,
Dad told me.
But there are skills
you'll need.
To make friends.
To get a job.

So I worked
with the coach.

I learned how to look
at someone's eyes
when I'm talking to them.
        Even when
        it makes me
        nervous.

How to take turns
in a conversation.
> Even when I just want
> to talk about physics.

How to answer
when someone asks,
How are you?
> How to say,
> *Fine.*
> Even when it's not true.

How are you?
Dr. Patel asks.

I duck my head
and tell him,
Fine.

Even though
my heart
is full of knots.

Even though
I can feel them
unraveling.

No Way

Niels looks up
when I walk into
the office.
He slides
his headphones
off his ears.
He smiles and says,
Hey.

For a moment,
my heart steadies.
Like the wind
dying down
after a storm.

Niels's eyes
swim.
From my shoulder
to my cheek.
From my cheek
to my chin.

Like he's connecting dots.
Like he's framing
my face.

*What are you
working on?*
I ask.

Niels smiles.
A flash of teeth.
Like a streetlight
blinking on.

History paper,
he says.

I frown.
I dart
a glance
at his laptop.

Don't you work
for your Dad?
I ask.

Niels shakes
his head.

No way,
he says.

I hate science.

My Whole Heart

Niels's words
settle
inside me.

And
my heart
tumbles.

Physics
is my
whole
life.

My whole
heart.

If Niels
doesn't like
physics,
then
he can't possibly
like me.

Not Like Me

Niels turns around.
He puts his headphones
back on.
He goes back
to his laptop.
Like I'm not
even
there.

My heart
crumples.

Niels is supposed to be
the one person
who understands me.

Someone with
challenges
like mine.

Someone with
stories
like mine.

But he's not like me.
And for the first time
in my life, I realize
I don't have anyone.

I'm completely
alone.

Out of Order

Tears burn
my throat.

I don't want to cry
in front of Niels.

So I spin around.
Looking for
somewhere to go.
Somewhere to run.

But as I turn,
my hand
hits
the stack of papers.

Dr. Patel's journal articles
come
       tumbling
           down.

They
slide
to the floor.

All
      out
of
      order.

And then
all the knots
inside me
come undone.
All at once.

And I slide
sideways.
Into the chair.

I clap my hands
over my eyes.

And I start
to cry.
And cry.
And cry.

Alone

I hear the squeak
of Niels's chair.

The clatter of
his headphones
on the desk.

The slap of his
sneakers
on the tile floor.

I hear him
walk out
of the office.

And then I'm really
truly
all
alone.

Back

A few minutes later,
Niels comes back.

I don't look up.
But I know
it's him.

I can tell by the soft pad
of his feet.
The way he clears
his throat.

He sets something
on the desk
in front of me.
I hear the flat sound of it
hitting the desk.

He crouches beside me.
Knees popping.

He doesn't say anything.
But I hear his breathing.
Soft and even.

What's Wrong?

When, at last,
I look up,
I see Niels.
Watching me.

He offers me
the box of tissues
he placed on my desk.
And then he rests his hand
on my chair.
Gently.
Like a drop of rain
landing
in an ocean.

His eyes
graze my forehead.
Feather light.

Mia,
he says.
What's wrong?

I'm Sorry

I tell
Niels,
I'm sorry.

But Niels shakes his head.
Dark lashes
brush his cheeks.
His eyes glitter.
Like a night full of stars.

He waves
his hand.
And he flicks
my apology
away.

Meltdown

Niels says that word.
Those two syllables.

Melt
          down.

And my heart
lifts.
Like the edge of a sail.

Tipping Over

When I got glue
on my fingers
in first grade,
I had
a meltdown.

My teacher called it
a tantrum.

But a meltdown
isn't the same thing
as a tantrum.

A meltdown
is an overloaded boat
that finally
        tips
                over.

A pressure cooker
that's been left
on the stove
for too long.

A meltdown
is my body's response
to too much
noise.

Too much
emotion.

Too
much.

Niels's gaze
brushes my hair.
Like a summer breeze.

And I realize
he may not like
science.

But he
understands.

I don't have to
explain.

And my insides
flicker
with warmth.

Like a
bonfire.

Like a
candle flame.

Favorite Place

Let's go to the lounge,
Niels says.

I wipe my eyes.
And then I force myself
to stand up.
To follow him
out the door.
Down the hallway.
Like I'm following
a thread
through a maze.

When we get
to the lounge,
he flops onto
one of the couches.
The leather creaks
and sighs
beneath him.
Like a house
settling.

Niels looks around.
His gaze sweeping across
the couches.
The vending machines.
The yellow walls.

I love it here,
he says.
This is
my favorite place.

His voice is
whispery.
Like the crush
of fallen leaves.

I thought you hated
science,
I say.

Niels tips his head
to one side.
He kicks out
his leg.
He taps my shoe
with his.

I hate science,
he says.

But I don't hate
scientists.

Some People

I look at Niels.
The soft curve
of his mouth.
The careful swing
of his eyes.
And I make
a decision.

I decide
to tell him
about the whispers
at school.
About my headphones.
Snatched away.

Niels's eyes
touch mine.
Briefly.
And then they
dart away.

I think of
fireflies.
Hummingbirds.

Of particles
bumping
into each other
in space.

Some people
will look at you,
he says.
And they will
only see
your autism.

But others
will see
a full picture.

A full
you.

I Hope

I don't know
Niels
the way I know
Chris.

I don't know
if he likes
grapes.
Or comic books.
Or algebra.

But I think
when Niels says
a full you,

he means
I see you.

I think
he's telling me
he understands.

I hope
he's saying
he's my friend.

Back in Place

Back in the office,
Niels and I
sit side by side
on the floor.

He hands me
journal articles.
One by one.

And I arrange them
in order.

Bit by bit,
we put the stack of
Dr. Patel's journal articles
back together.
Back in place.
Back where I found them.

Talk to Me

On the drive home
Dad's gaze
flicks
back and forth.
From me
to the road.
Like windshield wipers.
Like backyard swings.

I hold my breath
and wait.

And after a while,
Dad clears his throat.

Niña mía,
he says.
I know
something's wrong.

But I can't help you
if you don't
talk to me.

This Isn't Home

When I was a kid,
expressing feelings
was easier.

But as I got older,
I learned
to be strong.
To tie my feelings
up.
And keep them
to myself.

I look at Dad,
and I think of home.
Where nobody cared
if I wore headphones.
Nobody whispered.
Nobody stared.

Dad once told me
that crying
was how
I talked to him.
When I was a kid.
How I let him know
something
was wrong.

I don't want to cry
anymore.
But I don't want
to tie my feelings up
in knots
either.

So I take a deep breath.
I look at Dad.
And I say,
I don't like it here.

This isn't
anything
like home.

Home Isn't a Place

Dad guides the car
onto the highway.
Heading north.
Toward our new house.

Sunlight
bounces off his eyeglasses.
A wink and glimmer.
Steady.
Like a heartbeat.

Mia,
Dad says.
Home isn't a place.

It's a
feeling.

A
belonging.

Home
is where
you are
most
loved.

I don't know
if I understand that.

Are You Okay?

Chris texts me
right before bed.
Three words.
Are you okay?

I set my phone aside.
I look up at the ceiling.
And I think of Chris.
Tova.
Niels.

I think how some people
only see my autism.

But other people
see all of me.

I pick up my phone.
And I scroll back
through Chris's messages.

Before we moved
to Boston.
Before we left
Kansas City.

Conversations
about movie tickets.
Birthday parties.
Summer vacation.

They fill my screen.
Like echoes.
Like ghosts.

I scroll forward again.
Back to the present.
Back to here
and now.

I realize
I've brought all these
conversations
with me.
All the way
from Kansas City.

I've brought
Chris
with me.

I close my eyes.
And think of particles
bumping into each other.

How they
usually
spin away.

But sometimes,
they don't.

Sometimes, they form
a bond.

I Miss You

I text Chris back.
Three words.
I miss you.

And then,
I answer his question.

I tell him,
I'm not okay.

I Miss You, Too

The next morning,
I open my eyes.

I see
my big picture window.
My telescope.
Pointing up
at the sky.

And when I look down,
I see a message.
From Chris.

Hi Mia,
it says.
I miss you,
too.

It's okay
to not be
okay.

The Truth

I pick up
my phone.
And I tell Chris
the truth.

*I don't like it
here.
I'm not doing
great.*

> *You just got there.
> Give yourself time.*

*Everyone whispers
about me
at school.
I don't have
any friends.*

> *You've got me.*

But you're not here.

> *I'm right
> inside your phone.*

I start to tell him
that Mom
is disappointed
in me.

I can't do this
alone.
I don't know
how.

But then,
Chris says,
You figured out physics.
You figured out algebra.
You can figure this out,
too.

I Wish

I wish
I believed you.

> I know.
> I wish
> I could make you
> believe me.

I wish
we never moved.

> I wish
> I had a million dollars.

Haha!
I wish I had
some chocolate cake.

> I wish you knew
> how awesome
> you are.

Five Minutes to Spare

I'm still
texting Chris
when Mom walks in.

Mia!
she cries.
You're going to be late!

But I hop out of bed
before she can say
anything more.

I take
a quick shower.

I grab a
granola bar.

And I'm ready for school.
With five minutes to spare.

The New Kid

After first period,
Ms. Fray
calls me
to her desk.

I tell her
I don't want to be late
for English.

But she only
smiles.

I'll write you a pass,
she says.
*So you won't get
in trouble.*

She waits
for the room
to clear out.
Then,
she looks at me.
Her thin brows
form a V
over her eyes.

I know it's hard,
she says,
being the new kid.

I just want
to make sure
you're okay.

I take all my feelings.
And I gather them
together.
So I can
tie them up
in one big knot.

But then,
I think of Dad
telling me
he can't help me
if I don't talk.

Of Chris
telling me it's okay
to not be
okay.

Of feeling so alone
in this place I'm supposed
to feel most loved.

I don't have
any friends,
I tell Ms. Fray.

And I don't know
what to do
about it.

Friends

Ms. Fray tells me
it's hard for a lot of people
to make friends.
Not just me.

*How did you make friends
at your old school?*
she asks.

I don't know,
I admit.

I tell her
about Chris.
About how
he
found
me.

And then I tell her
about physics club.

Well,
Ms. Fray sighs,
*there's no
physics club
here . . .*

*But that doesn't mean
we can't start one.*

I Didn't Know

I'm late
to second period.

But I hand
my pass
to Ms. Levin.

She starts to wave me
toward my chair.
But then she stops.
She crooks her finger
at me.
And drops her voice.

Mia,
she says.
*I'm sorry
about your headphones.
I didn't know.*

I nod
and tell her
it's okay.

There are a lot of things
people don't understand
about autism.

There are a lot of things
people don't know.

Something Else Entirely

I open
my textbook
to another poem.
More words
that don't rhyme.

Ms. Levin
reads it out loud.
And I think of Mom
sitting in bed beside me.
The poems
she used to read
at bedtime.
Silly words
bouncing like rubber balls
between us.

Ms. Levin finishes reading.
And then she presses her palms
together.

*This is one
of my favorite
poems,*
she says.

*Can anyone
guess
why?*

Silence
hangs over the classroom.
Thick as fog.

Someone
calls out,
Because it's a short one!
And the classroom
bubbles over
with laughter.

Ms. Levin laughs, too.
But then,
she shakes her head.

This is my favorite poem,
she says.
Because it speaks to me.

It reminds me of things
the poet
probably
never intended.

She leans forward.
Hands gripping
the edge of her desk.

That's the thing
about poetry,
she says.

It can be
about one thing.
But it can
make you think about
something
different.

It can say
one thing.

But mean
something else
entirely.

Announcement

During third period,
the speaker crackles.

Ms. Fray's voice
comes on.
Tinny and distorted.

*We're starting
a new club,*
she announces.
A science club.

*Anyone interested
in joining
can meet me
at lunchtime.*

A Minute

At lunchtime,
I head
straight
for the biology room.

But when I walk in,
the room is
empty.
Except for Ms. Fray.

Have a seat,
she says.
*We'll give
the others
a minute.*

*Not everyone
is as quick
as you are.*

Apple

I sit at my desk.
Hands folded.

Go ahead and eat,
Ms. Fray says.
This is a
working lunch.

I reach
in my backpack
and pull out
my lunch bag.

I open it.

And then,
I freeze.

There's no bag of grapes
inside.

Instead,
I find
an apple.
Crunchy
and
crisp.

Two Girls

Ten minutes
into lunch,
Tova
walks in.
Dark hair spilling
over her shoulders.
Like a waterfall.

She's with
a girl
I don't know.
Someone
I've never seen
before.

They don't see me
sitting at my desk.
But I
see them.

Rumor

Ms. Fray tells them
to take a seat.

So they turn
and look over
the empty chairs.

Tova's eyes catch mine.
And her cheeks turn pink.

She sucks in
a breath.
She straightens
her shoulders.
And then she grabs
her friend's arm.
She tugs her forward.
Right toward me.

Hi, Mia,
Tova says.
*I think I owe you
an apology.*

*I heard a rumor
about you
that wasn't true.*

*And I didn't say
anything.*

A Part of Me

Autism
is a part of me.
Like having brown hair.
Like loving physics.
Like hating grapes.

It's a part of me.
And I choose
to share it.

I choose
to shake my head.
And say,
The rumor was true.

I'm
autistic.

About Autism

Tova's pink-glossed lips
fall open.

Her friend blinks at me.
For two seconds.
Four.
Eight.

After a while
I sigh.

And then I tell them
about autism.

About
the
rainbow.

I explain it to them.
Just like Dad did
when I was eight.

Science Club

Science club
isn't like
physics club.

Only the three of us
show up.

But we spend
the entire lunch
talking about
science.
I say maybe we can
do a field trip
to the MIT lab,
and they're excited!

When lunch is over,
Tova offers
to walk
with me
to my locker.

Her friend tells me
her name is
Natalie.
And she offers
to come, too.

The three of us
walk down the hall.
Our textbooks
in our hands.

We don't say
a word.
But we walk
together.

Side
by
side.

Mia Mía

That night
Mom knocks
on the door.
Quick and light.
Like rain
pattering
on a window.

She sinks down
onto the bed.
Right beside me.
Just like
she used to.
When I was a kid.

Mia mía,
she says.

My
Mia . . .

Because I'm Afraid

Mom rakes both hands
through her loose curls.

Mia mía,
she says.
*You said something
yesterday
that took my breath away.*

She smooths her skirt
around her knees
and sighs.

*You said
you have to stop
being you.*

I open my mouth
to defend myself.
To explain.

But Mom
shakes her head.

*I'm sorry
if I've made you feel
like you're not doing enough,*
she says.

You are beautiful.
Just the way you are.

You are
enough.

When I push you
to be stronger,
it's because I worry.
Because I'm afraid.

I don't want you
to suffer.

I don't want you
to be hurt.

I love you
more than anything
in this whole world.

What You Need

I lie in bed
long after Mom leaves.

I close my eyes.
And I make a list
of the things
Mom says to me.

1. You have to be brave.
2. You have to be strong.

I open my eyes.
And I make another list.
About what she means.

1. I worry about you.
2. I want you to be happy.
3. I love you.

I run
back over
my lists
in my head.

And I think about
words.
Poems.

How they can say one thing.
But mean something else entirely.

Smooth and Dependable

I open my eyes
the next morning.
And the first thing I do
is pull out my phone.

I tell Chris
about Mom.
About Niels.
About Tova.
About Ms. Fray.

He tells me
about his new
algebra tutor.

When Mom walks in,
I hop out of bed.
I take a quick shower.
I grab a granola bar.

I follow my new routine.
Like a line on a map.
Like a freshly paved road.

Smooth
and
dependable.

In My Heart

Mom is waiting
in the car
to drive me to school.

So I run out of the house.
With five minutes
to spare.

As we pull away,
I look back.

I see my big
picture window.
The wraparound porch.
The wind chime
we brought with us
from Kansas.

I think about
how Mom once said,
Home is where the heart is.

I think about
how Dad once said,
Home is a feeling.
Home is where
you are most loved.

Maybe they're both saying
the same thing
two different ways.

Maybe it'll take a while for me
to know what home means
for me.

Maybe home is less like science,
more like poetry.

Leaving Kansas City
was the hardest thing
I've ever had to do.
I had to leave behind
everything I knew.

But I brought
my heart with me.
The place I carry Mom.
And Dad.
And Chris.

And I can make room in it
for other people
and experiences.

Maybe as long as I have
my own special heart,
and keep it open,
I'll always be
home.

WANT TO KEEP READING?

If you liked this book, check out another
book from West 44 Books:

TO BE MAYA
BY CLAUDIA RECINOS SELDEEN

ISBN: 9781978596191

What It Means to Be Maya

The Mayan people once lived
all
      over
            Central America.

They built temples
      out of stone.

They made knives
      out of flint.

They made jewelry
      out of jade.

They carved their life
      out of the jungle.

They were fierce and proud.

My mother named me Maya
to connect me
      to my past.

And to Guatemala.
    The country where she was born.
    The country she left
    five years
    before I came along.

She named me Maya
for the Mayan people,
our ancestors.

But I am not fierce.
I am not stone
    or flint
    or jade.

I am just a girl.
And my name is my own.

Claudia Recinos Seldeen

CATCH ME IF I
Fall

THE SONG I'M IN

Sick Girl
Secrets

Anna Russell

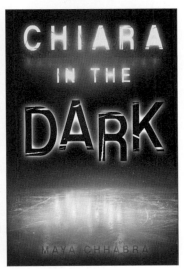

CHIARA IN THE DARK

MAYA CHHABRA

CHECK OUT MORE BOOKS AT:

www.west44books.com

About the Author

Claudia is the author of the young adult novels *To Be Maya* and *Catch Me If I Fall*. Her work has appeared in *The Amphibian Literary Journal* and *First Peoples Shared Stories*. Claudia is a first-generation Guatemalan American. When not writing, she is either playing video games with her husband and son, or flying through the air on a trapeze. Find out more at www.recinosseldeen.com.